CATRINA D. BROWN

STILL2CUM

Sequel to the Highly Acclaimed

.CUM

I0592636

CATRINA BROWN

STILL2CUM

Trixie Publications

557 Hoxie Avenue

Calumet City, Illinois 60409

To the best of said publisher's knowledge, this is an original manuscript and is the sole property of the author known as **CATRINA BROWN.**

Published by: **TRIXIE PUBLICATIONS** 2018

Printed by Ingram Spark 2018

ISBN: 978-0-692-09725-0

Printed in the United States of America

DEDICATION

I thank God for the many blessings He has given me in this cruel game called Life. I'm so grateful it's beyond words. Who would have ever thought it would go this far?

I want to thank my 3 sons, my ride or dies, Justin, Alonzo, and Russell for loving and believing in me. I want to thank my guardian angel, my daughter Jade Alexis. Continue to rest as you are among some great people. I want to thank my granddaughter Jade Amena for keeping me on my toes.

I want to my mom Gwendolyn for creating and molding me into the woman I am today. I know my brothers Istosh and Johnny are within my heart wishing physically you could enjoy this moment with me. I want to thank my brother Tyas for being supportive in more ways than one.

I want to thank my old diehard friends, you know who you are, as well as my new friends.

I want to thank each and everyone one who has supported my dream. I am so happy my new and old fans are enjoying my book series, t-shirts and other projects I'm mixing up as I speak.

Love you all and again thank you.

INTRODUCTION

I have frequented an online dating site off and on for over four years. Within that time, I became engaged. Due to it not working out, my journey continued as I earned my PHD in online dating, LOL!!!

I have encountered drivers, preachers, shysters, bosses, actors, blasts from past, musicians, and jerks of all sizes. The owners of these sites are the real **PIMPS**. They are making all the money by setting the platforms for people all over the world to meet in various forms; via phone, text, video chat, or some in person. Regardless, to view profiles is free but to read and view your messages is how the pimps get paid.

My overall experience has been knowledgeable, fun, sad, loving, and rewarding. I've met some great people and some not so great, but I look at all my experiences as

lessons. He is preparing me for the one I deserve. Did I

meet him or didn't I? Get your snacks!

Chapter 1

2016...

This time around my focus has completely changed, mentally and physically. My search has become more spiritual. I'm becoming more aware of my alcohol intake (rest in peace Trixie), and my attitude. Besides, I am getting older. I am not in control. God has this and He knows who's best for me. I'm on the passenger side and He's driving this car. I am building these lessons for my new husband or partner so I can be the best wife or partner I can be. I feel all I need is one good man; although a lot of women say there are no good men out here. I beg to differ.

Some men are facing some of the same drama as we women. They have been cheated on, lied to, abused and broken just as we have. Some have more baggage than the average woman is said to have. However, there is hope. Since the post office and UPS aren't delivering men to my door, online dating was my outlet.

People ask if I'm scared to meet people in person especially those who live in other states. They say there are weirdos and perverts who use online dating. That may be true but you have to step out on faith, take chances in life and use discernment when connecting. You could be in a relationship with someone for many years and there is a possibility they could say or do things to you that you wouldn't have ever thought possible. My question is, who do we really know? Here I am, throwing my craps on the table again, hoping I don't get snake eyed or crap out, LMAO!!!

Chapter 2

At that point in my life, I was in a dark place. Always making everyone else happy but not making Trina happy. I started self-medicating and withdrawing from the world. Missing work, not socializing with anyone, content with being by myself and finding much needed self-peace.

Once my hiatus was over, I jumped back in the dating ring and met Clyde, Mr. Alpha Male. He lived in a suburb in Illinois, was 46, vice president of a security firm, a private investigator, and owned his own home. We had identical cars. He was 6', built like a brick wall and fine as hell! Only set back was he had 2 dogs and we all know I am terrified of dogs, so keep your fingers crossed.

We began chatting on and off the site; our conversations were very pleasant. We'd have the usual "get to know you" talks but what threw me for a loop was when he stated..

"I'm glad you are giving me the time of day." I was lost.

He went on to say he'd tried talking to me a few months ago but I blew him off after a few messages. Now I was really lost because in my right mind, I wouldn't have passed his fine ass up.

Chapter 3

I'm not a mean-spirited person. I don't know if I was in a relationship with someone else at that time or just doing some self-reflecting. I apologized to him as a gesture of respect.

Whenever someone leaves me a written message and not one generated, I make it my business to respond.

We continued conversations through written messages for the next few weeks. Afterwards, we exchanged numbers to get to know each other a little better. We didn't talk on the phone right away and honestly, I didn't remember who he was because I was talking to other people from the site as well. My slick ass asked him for a picture. He text me back that he didn't like sending pictures because he didn't really know me. I sent one to break the ice and kept up the charade that I knew him. After the picture exchange, we finally decided to meet.

For our first date, we met at a winery. He was just as fine in person as his profile picture. Mmmmmm. Our dinner was great and our chemistry was greater.

He revealed he was a private investigator, which helped me understand the need for all the secrecy. We laughed at each other's jokes although he asked too many damn questions. For a minute, I thought I was in a psychiatrist's chair! LOL. But we enjoyed dinner and our wine tasting, peeling back one layer at a time the more we conversed. We parted ways, excited about our new friendship and ready for our next date.

The following weeks, we talked and text daily, checking on each other due to our professions. You know I'm a thinker so I knew one of our issues would be his 2 big ass dogs. For our second date, we planned to meet at a friend's party then spend the rest of the evening together, once he arrived.

As the night went on, he finally called, said he was parking and would be on his way inside. Another 20 minutes went by and I called him. He said he left because it was too crowded plus it looked like I was already having a good time. **Hold the presses**! This muthafucka watched me at the party the whole time, didn't say a word, saw me talking to a co-worker and assumed the worst? The joke was on him. LMAO!!! P.S. The co-worker was gay. **Unbelievable!**

Now my mind was going in circles thinking I'm going to have to watch over my shoulder at all times. I better not give this nigga my social or he would know all the shit, LOL!

Chapter 4

"No matter what event or family function we attend together, I need your undivided attention at all times. I'm selfish." This is what he told me a few days after the incident.

Uurrrrrrrrgghhh! Not talking to anyone at a party and dealing with the fact that he wasn't a people person was a deal-breaker. He had lost his fuckin' mind! I couldn't focus on anyone but him? Hasta la vista, baby. "Click."

Day one, no Clyde, day two, I definitely knew it was over. In the time that had passed, we'd had plans for a paint date. Those plans and any other for our future was a bust. So when he text me out of the blue, I was shocked.

With him being the 'alpha male' and 'king of the jungle', I thought I'd never hear from him again.

He sent me the picture I'd originally sent him saying he missed my pretty face and if his contacting me was going to be a problem, he wouldn't call or text again. We missed each other and blamed it on miscommunication. His choosing to break down to contact me meant everything because he was so arrogant.

On our next date, we met at the winery again. He said he couldn't believe I thought he'd never call again. I told him..

"I'm a runner with my Nike's on at all times."

"The reason you were so quick to give up is because you don't know me..." Those were his words. BOOM!!!

We ended the date with our first kiss. My heart skipped and the taste of his sweet tongue was more than delicious. I desired the softness of his lips; they felt like cotton candy melting in my mouth. The light touch of his fingertips along my neckline was so sensual.

Our breathing was on one accord as we twirled each other's tongues like a merry-go-round. I sucked his tongue in and out my mouth like I was sucking his dick. We put it on pause, which was best, before we ended up in somebody's hotel room.

I was looking forward to seeing how far we could go or would he be my final chapter. Plus, I was just giving him a sample of what he could have had. Too bad, so sad. I was going to a coworker's event and asked him to join me. He was working, of course. I decided not to go and stayed home, not letting him know anything different.

Chapter 5

He called and called, I never answered. That Negro was some kinda mad at me. He left me a voicemail, telling me that since I'm too busy to answer, to go with and spend my birthday trip with the person whose face I was in! I was cracking up as his insecurity showed me that whatever he accused me of, he was doing all along.

The next day when we talked he was still accusing me of wrongdoing, so I did the Jedi mind trick on his ass. I told him to continue being with ole girl.

He said, "Who?"

I played it off like I really knew there was someone else. Eventually he told on himself and I tricked his dumb ass with his own words. Got 'em. I should have gotten him a t-shirt made to read, 'No Bitchassness'. LMAO!!!

Then there was Aaron claiming to be 49, but I knew he was older. I let it slide, plus he had the cutest deep dimples. We talked on the phone for a week or so and met at the same winery establishment. We stood at the bar for wine tastings. He was okay, but not for me. The meeting ended sooner rather than later when he tried to rub my thigh. I told him..

"You don't know me, so don't touch me."

"I'm trying to get to know you but you won't help a brother out." That was his weak ass response.

I sipped the last of my wine, turned on my heels and told him to kiss my ass. I found out later that he was a gotdamn preacher. SMH. Trying to spend the congregation's tithes on some ass.

Chapter 6

New York in the house! Lonnie, originally from 'The Big Apple', relocated to Texas for love. We met online on a Sunday. I loved his voice, but physically he was on the short side but was easy on the eyes.

He explained he grew up with this chick and they had been friends for years and lost contact. They reconnected after some time. He had gotten into some problems and she told him to pack up everything and move to Texas so they could start a life together. When he got there, it was a whole different scenario. She was already married then played 'amnesia' and left his ass out in the cold, not knowing anyone. *Damn*, I thought I had it bad. He found a shelter, got a job and began to rebuild his life in Texas.

We"d only talked for a few days before he was trying to wife a sister. Hold up, wait a minute! He was crazy as hell! He didn't want me to talk to anyone. I was his woman, and I had to be loyal no matter what. I'm like, this fool is retarded. We talked for 2 days and he got mad when I didn't answer right away. The warning bells went off on high alert and I just knew he wasn't serious but... shit, he was. I had to remind him I was the Queen of Blocking. Boop! Be gone. That month must have been the time for possessive psychos.

Marty was next. He constantly left messages on my page every other month for years. I didn't want to be a bitch knowing physically he definitely wasn't my type, looking like Supafly from the 70's. It didn't take me long, 2 conversations, to see he was a 53-year-old certified nut. I'm still on the lookout for a man with a perm, a cape and platforms. LOL!!!

Chapter 7

Nut #3 was Dwight from Ohio, 47, about 5'8, employed, owned his own home and had an adult daughter he adored. I was keeping an open mind. Remember God is driving this car, so we talked and exchanged pictures for a few weeks and decided to meet in person.

The original plan was for him to drive up, get a room and we were going out on the town. As luck would have it, he couldn't get off work blah, blah, blah, so I told him I would make the trip for real. I considered it. He had bought champagne, cooked dinner and bought gifts. I was leaving on a Sunday, going for a day but he turned me off during our last conversation.

"Could you go by the liquor store and buy me a bottle of Absolute because it's probably cheaper in Illinois."

In my mind, how have you bought all these things for me and you can't afford a bottle for your damn self? No way Jose; it was over before it began.

After the fact, his birthday came and he was pissed I didn't get him a card or gift. Idiot, I don't even know you, let's keep it that way. Hasta la vista, baby…

Chapter 8

Roberto from New York, was 6'0, handsome, a business owner and pervert. He had hit my box numerous times throughout the years with small talk; I wasn't sure if I wanted a long distance friendship. He was so persistent, I finally had a private chat conversation with him.

Second thing he says was, "I'm getting out the shower, I wish you were here..." That's a no-no!

Rule #1, don't talk under my clothes. I'm not on the line for sex, I'm not a prostitute.

I responded back with, "you are barking up the wrong tree. I'm on the site to get to know someone's heart, not their dick size." He apologized and we exchanged numbers.

During our first and last conversation he was constantly yelling at other drivers, the people, complaining about everything while we were on the phone; we couldn't even have a decent conversation.

In between the yelling, he would ask what I was wearing, or did I like to kiss or be choked. I knew he wasn't the one for me.

Now Stoney, 47, 6'3, and 355 lbs. from Michigan, was a straight clown…

He owned 2 profitable establishments, was the father of 3 and a youth football coach with the physique of a linebacker; big muscles with a big head to match.

He was cool to talk to at first. I was out of town when we spoke for the first time. I was in party mode and to be honest, I didn't remember half of our conversation, so I had to wing it.

When I returned home, we talked more one I sobered up.. LOL! He really wasn't so bad to talk to after all.

Our talks lasted a few more weeks but he clowned me and hurt my feelings (I do have feelings, LMAO!). He had an issue with me still being on the site.

These were his words to me, "When we initially started talking, you should have automatically gotten off the site because you and me are together…"Errrrghhh!!! I didn't get that memo so I told him..

"My subscription doesn't expiring for another 30 days. I check *my* messages on *my* paid online page whenever I get a notification." Jeez Louise!

After going back and forth, our agreement was we'd both see where this could go and take it one day at a time. **(Please note: How did he know I was still online if he wasn't on there his damn self?).** Stop playing with me!

I went along with his games for entertainment purposes until his insecurities got old and stale.

Chapter 9

Manny from Memphis popped on my line, stating after reading my profile..

"It sounds like you need a southern gentleman in my life..." I thought it was catchy, so I looked at his profile pictures and information before responding. It looked like he was popular in the music industry. He had a lot of past and current pictures with celebrities at different functions.

I responded with a smiley face: however, he apologized, telling me he was off the market. I was confused, wondering why he's on a dating site. He stated he'd catered a function (I guess he is a chef too) and spoke to some single colleagues, and wondered if I was interested in attending a meet and greet with successful single people like myself, it was for an event he was putting together.

My initial response was, "NO! I'm not flying to Memphis for no shit like that!" I declined and gave him my blessings.

Yet, as I sat and thought more about the idea, a light bulb came on in my mind. I thought, h*e is pimping the PIMPS.* LOL! He is setting up dates for people on the dating site in Memphis. Well, I'll be damned. As you can imagine, my attending the event never happened...

Next, for a brief moment, and when I say brief, I mean brief, there was Chad from Virginia. Tall, chocolate, and handsome. His attire in his pictures was really nice. I love for a man to dress and smell good.

We chatted back and forth for a few days. He was respectful, so we exchanged numbers. We talked on the phone a couple of times, and his conversation was sharp, just like his taste in clothing. I sent him a picture of me fully dressed and he said he would send me one in return.

This Negro had the audacity to send me a video of him

masturbating. I was offended to the 10th power. Ironically,

his 2 minutes of fame was of over in an instant.

Chapter 10

I have learned to accept that the Lord allows people in your life for a reason, so I am open to finding out why. Due to this, when I come in contact with someone, I'm not initially sure if he's the one, a crank or a creep. Maybe the Lord is showing me who not to deal with and their shenanigans.

When men reach out from other states, I never know if he could be the one for me. I'm open to relocating to somewhere warmer for true love. The most flirts and messages I have received are from the eastern states: New York, New Jersey, Virginia, Maryland, Philadelphia and even a couple from Rhode Island. They love my blonde hair.

On the flip side you have to use common sense and intuition normally. You get a feeling after the first couple of conversations. I will bow out gracefully and give them my blessings to whomever is for them, but it's not ME.

It's okay, I can accept if I'm not someone's type, my attitude stinks, or I'm too crazy; but what I can't accept is disrespect, disloyalty or just a plain ole liar.

Chapter 11

Speaking of liars, up to bat was Peter. We talked initially 2 months prior. He would text me poems daily and requested my presence on numerous occasions. I thought he was full of shit and wasn't a bit impressed but I wasn't rude. He would brag about his material possessions; his homes, and the great assets he could bring to the table. His poetry and conversation was off the chain and I give credit when it is due.

He was a native New Yorker , 5'11, stocky, a Biggie Smalls look alike, and had the gift of gab. For months we would entertain each other daily, promising to have a face-to-face meeting in whatever state was convenient, at his expense of course. He claimed I was the one.

He would say shit like..

"I'm your King. Please allow me to treat you as the Queen you are." With promises of a New York view, champagne, strawberries and the time of my life.

Me, being me, hopped on a plane with the intentions of making some New York memories and having my back blown out with a kool-aid smile.

However, the day I left for New York, everything that could go wrong went wrong. Flat tire on my car, my phone was acting up, I almost missed my flight, and when I landed in New York, there was a malfunction with the plane and we had to sit there for an extra 45 minutes. I should have taken heed to the signs. Don't go to the light Carol Ann, LOL!!! I should have jumped my ass off the plane and ran down the runway like I was running for the border, LMAO!

When I arrived at the condo, in the Bronx, around the corner from Yankee Stadium, I was not impressed. Their overpriced apartments were designed like the project buildings in Chicago. As much money as he'd paid to rent it, $350 per night was ridiculous. Bullshit!

The interior of the place was nice, clean and definitely had a beautiful view of the city at night. He greeted me with open arms and was dressed very nicely, smelled good, and he was so fine, I let out the breath I'd been holding since leaving for the airport. I could breathe again. Wheeeeeeew!...Woosahhhh! With champagne and wine, gifts, plus lunch waiting for me, I was a happy camper.

We planned to catch the train into Manhattan the next day because it was freezing outside. We spent the afternoon talking and sipping cocktails while getting better acquainted with each other. It was cool until we started talking about sex.

Now let me remind you, prior to meeting, he had

sent me pictures of his anaconda, I mean "DICK." It was

the blackest, longest, monstrosity I'd ever seen and I have

to admit, I was not looking forward to wrestling that

monster, LOL! Sex was the last thing on my agenda. I just

wanted to enjoy him and New York.

"Whatever you want, I'll do. Even if you want to

piss or shit on me, baby I'm down..." That was his promise

and I was like HUH?!!

I played it off but in my mind I was like *What the*

fuck?! This was the craziest shit I'd ever heard. LMAO!!!

He removed my shoes and socks and began

massaging my feet; and before I knew it, he was sucking

my toes and was good at it. I didn't know if it was the wine

or the lack of male attention, but I was turned the fuck on.

Unfortunately, between the food and wine, I was

full as hell and my gut was doing a number one me. So,

before I made a fool of myself, I excused myself to the bathroom. Soon as I closed the door, I started spilling my guts. I was so embarrassed, trying to keep it on the low and praying he didn't hear me from the other room.

Once I got myself together and showered, I changed into my pajamas, rejoining him in the living room like nothing ever happened. I was tired from the early morning flight, tipsy, and still dizzy so calling it a night was my best option. Plus, I already told you I was a little scared of the snake, LOL! He snored like a fuckin' bull. He must have been just as tired as I was. He called those hogs all night so I got no rest on the farm.

Morning came with him whispering, "We fuckin' today?"

I put on my big girl panties and thoughts of riding that horse became a reality sooner rather than later. He went for the gold. He started by sucking my chocolate nipples and rubbing my pussy into a creamy lather. He trailed my body with his wet kisses, bringing my body to life every place he touched.

He slurped and tugged on my clit ever so softly, with just a little pressure, in a circular motion until I popped off my first nut. Damn it felt so good! I had been reserving my pussy for a while, waiting patiently for a well-deserving gentleman to get his reward.

He kept licking, not knowing if I would cum again; he was rough. His facial hair was prickly and his kisses were even a rough dynamic. I thought I tasted blood at one point. However, a gentleman he truly was.

He put no pressure on me for sex. I told him I was hesitant because of his size and he respected my wishes to wait until later that not.

We got dressed and headed out to Manhattan. I can honestly say we had a great day. We went to the movies, sight-seeing, shopping, dinner at one of my favorite restaurants, and hung out in Time Square. It was the funniest thing. We walked around New York looking like Biggie and Faith, LOL! Me with my platinum blonde hair and him big, black, and wearing Versace shades, wearing matching black mink coats, LMAO! We took a break from the winter cold and went inside to chit chat for a while.

Chapter 12

We took turns expressing what we honestly thought of one another so far. He said I had a bad attitude and would make negative facial expressions but he could deal with it. I tried to explain to him I was very passionate and didn't mind expressing myself. It's called communication, that's what adults do. You sit down, hash it out, find a solution and keep it moving. I told him he continuously made himself appear more than he was.

Some of his claimed accomplishments were being a millionaire, fashion designer and top Chef. Oh, and don't let me forget, a well-known representative for a record label. I'm not a hater and those are great things. I give credit when it is due but the proof is in the pudding. The bragging was a huge turn off. Overall, it was a great date.

On our way back to the condo, we stopped at the liquor store for champagne and I was told it was good. This Negro had the nerve to get mad and stopped talking to me because I didn't want to drink anymore with him. I had a flight to catch the next day, so I just wanted to chill.

We got back to the house and I started getting my things together for my afternoon departure. Lord knows I was ready to go. He'd started getting on my nerves by asking over and over..

"What are we going to do?" He claimed he really liked me and even felt some love towards me. He stated with our distance; him living in L.A. and me in Chicago, he wanted to know where we stood and where we could go from here. He felt if we continued to visit each other, someone would have to relocate. WTF!!! This muthafucka was acting like it was an invasion of the body snatchers. Where did he come from? LMAO!!! Nigga please..

I went with the motion and I was very proud of myself because I held my tongue and was peaceful, knowing this little episode was almost over.

As we continued talking, guy inserted some foreplay. He went straight for my welcoming pussy because some good head, I would never turn down and would get some act right A.S.A.P.

As he was licking, he asked,

"Where's your clit? It's so small…"

"Have you ever been to Africa where they cut the women's clits off?" I was like Jodeci at that point, Don't talk, just listen. LMAO!

He pulled out his dick and it wasn't as huge as I'd originally thought. He forgot to list one helluva photographer as one of his accomplishments, LOL!!!!

I gave him some "you're going to miss this good ass pussy... here's one for the road" type pussy. He had a nice piece of wood though, I'm not going to lie.

I laid him on his back, he put that Magnum condom on and it was time to ride the bull. I teased his ass by putting it in inch by inch while gripping his dick with my suction cup, my walls giving him pleasure every second. I was rolling and grinding on his dick, letting it slide in and out. Man, he didn't know if he was going or coming! I sat up straight, letting his dick go deep inside. Lights out! He came, yelling so loud I thought I'd broken it, LOL! Us both being sexually satisfied and the long day we'd had, aided in giving us a restful night's sleep.

Chapter 13

I woke up the next morning and surprisingly, he gone out and bought me breakfast. I thought to myself, *Either he is glad my ass is leaving or he really enjoyed our night together.* I know I am a handful that's why I didn't want to drink. That would have made "Trixie" get with his freaky ass but I wasn't feeling him like that.

Overall, he was respectful, a gentlemen, but not for me. Besides, the distance was an issue. Not sure if I wanted another long distance relationship.

A few hours before I leave, he goes in the bathroom and takes a little while so I'm thinking he was taking a dump. Suddenly, I start receiving numerous videos from him showing his different homes, cars, and his new business venture that was going to take him back to the top.

When he came out, I had this confused look on my face, so he then hands me this beat up 5 X 7 photo book of models wearing his designs. I thought he was pathetic. Material things made him.

Now don't get me messed up, I'm happy for anyone who's successful but not constantly talking about it like material possessions run your life. I decided to give him a little of my prized possession so he could remember ole hurricane. By now I wasn't tired and sober.

He pulled out his dick as I proceeded to bent over, grabbing my ankles. He grabbed my hips and went to work. We came together then embraced each other as if we were one... that was the most peaceful moment of silence we'd shared during the entire trip.

I showered, got dressed, got my shit, and split; didn't want to miss my plane. We went out to get a taxi. As he was loading my bags he kept asking,

"When am I going to see you again?"

I answered simply, "I don't know."

He told me he loved me and asked me if I was going to marry him. I replied with, "I have to go, I'm running late. We will talk soon. Thank you for a great New York experience."

As I landed in my city, I sent him a goodbye text. I told him he shouldn't belittle or talk down to people because they make less than him. I let him know I made it home and thanked him again. I also told him to sit back, rewind and understand that some of the things he says and does are harmful. He told me he loved me and that we are on two different financial levels and he felt I couldn't keep up with him. I totally agreed and wished him the best. I couldn't give him anymore of my attention and I couldn't

be bought....Peace.

This man still calls/text every week, asking me to

meet him in different cities as he travels so we can sit down

and get us on the same page. We are still friends or distant

ships sailing through the night. He has a good heart but that

millionaire mentality SUCKS!!!

Chapter 14

Tommy, a minister from Mississippi, put his bet in on meeting Missy. During our first conversation, he told me he had a radio show that airs on Fridays with a Chicagoan. This person had a similar name to the so- called faceless author that I wrote about in my last book. He's the faceless man that would never show his real self or a current picture. Hmmm...

I was definitely on alert and turned off because I was thinking they ran in the same circles playing games. I knew I wasn't going to talk to him anymore. It was some bullshit in the mix.

He called me every week leaving messages or texts, until one day I finally gave in and talked to him. I asked him if I could be honest, he said yes. I explained to him the similarities/story line he had with someone else. I also put emphasis on the fact that I didn't have time to play games. He understood why I avoided him and assured me he didn't know the man at all. We started over and began to talking daily, getting to know each other. He said he had been a pastor for the past 20 years, a father and a divorcee; he also worked in the auto industry.

Our conversations were interesting. He made me feel like I was always on an interview. He spoke of ministry highly and revealed to me I was a blessed person with blessings all around me. He could get a little thuggish at times, he was no punk but truly a man of God.

We video chatted and I was pleased. He was a little taller than I, solidly built with a nonsense personality. I would stop myself from using certain curse words out of respect. I was confused when I received a few pictures with him only in a towel. Daannngggg Rev. LMAO!!! I thought I was being set up and I didn't want to play in those reindeer games. I told him they were nice but totally unexpected, just speechless.

He told me one day he wanted to say certain things but couldn't because he was a minister. He would have his cousin call and tell me what he was thinking or wanted to say. I told him he was a grown ass man and whatever he had to say to me, *he'd* better say it. That made me feel some kind of way because what type of bullshit in the game was this.

One night ole pastor was feeling freaky and wanted to play. But I wouldn't feed into it or would change the subject and just disregard his "blessings". Other than that, he was nice, respectful, and encouraging.

But note... the truth will come to the light. LOL! We became social media friends, which was cool, and it was one of our late night phone rendezvous that ended on a happy note.

After the call, I made a comment on his page..

"Night night Rev." I heard "crickets" it was so quiet and I didn't hear from him for a few days. This was out of the ordinary for him; this man called/text every day. I figured maybe he had one of the sisters from the church on his page or a little something on the side and he stopped talking to me. I checked to see if he'd deleted me but that wasn't the case.

Finally, I received a picture of him in a hospital bed and asked what had happened. He said he was sick and in pain. Now, I felt a little bad thinking he was caught up over my message.

In the following days, we text here and there, but it wasn't the same. I was probably right, he had to slow his roll. Since he was a decent guy, we still talk sparingly and only the Lord really knows the truth.

Chapter 15

I don't know what it was about these preachers, I just couldn't shake them. Now here comes Pastor Clyde from Minneapolis on deck. He was 5'11, stocky, with no kids. We talked and connected, realizing we were the same zodiac sign. He was outgoing, very spiritual, and ambitious. He had his own youth foundation, empowering and mentoring people in his city. He was a writer, teacher, and a prayer warrior who prayed for me every time we ended our conversations. I enjoyed that about him.

As we began to learn more about each other, he opened my eyes a little more about the strength and power of prayer. We had talked about eventually meeting in person but his downfall was he could be very critical and judgmental. He acted as if he was my father at times and we would go back and forth so I knew it wouldn't last. The

last straw was when he judged my book title, yet had never

read my book. I gave him my resignation and said bye-bye

to being the 'first lady.' LOL!

Chapter 16

Mr. Ramon, one of my co-workers for years was a nice, respectful, Latin man and very easy on the eyes. Not that race plays a part; a man is a man. Color is not a factor as long as he treats me nice, that's the objective.

When he saw me on the site, he messaged me asking, "What are doing on here?"

"The same reason you on here, trying to find a date." We both laughed and got a kick out of it.

I asked him, "Any luck?"

He said, "No, it's a bunch of liars, game players, and women trying to get men to pay their bills for some pussy."

I understood wholeheartedly! I didn't get the concept of some people wasting their time and money or even just trying to get over on others. I assumed everyone on the site was an adult. They should have a way where you can find out if they are on some bullshit or not.

He left me his number and said if I wanted to hang out, give him a call. I personally think he's a great guy but he dated someone I know. One of my number one rules is, I don't date or mess around with someone I know. Not even if they are someone I was friends with at some point in my life. Homey don't play that.

Chapter 17

I had to reach way back to the very beginning. He should have been in my first book. Judais, a handsome Nigerian native, residing in New York. He's a father, employed, and a die-hard Catrina fan. I've been corresponding with this man for over 4 years on and off. He has been consistent; my love, and my true friend. He would send me bible scriptures and poems on the site for months. He was never disrespectful and never talked under my clothes. We would check in on each other on the site from time to time. In our first year, we basically just spoke or gave each other blessings and encouragement.

We somehow got reconnected and no matter how much time passed, we continued talking as if we had talked the day before. This year we have connected more in video chats and the phone. His accent is so thick I have to look at his lips to truly understand what he's saying. But the current year he has turned up the heat sending me porn videos. I told him I was shocked because we never talked sex and I asked him where this was coming from? He apologized and we went back to the PG conversations, LOL! He's been asking me to visit but my 'Spidey' senses are telling me, *No, that's one trip you don't have to make.*

He talks of watching over me while I sleep when I come visit. Urrrrrrrrrgghhhhh! That creeped me out. I have been to New York plenty of times but we don't seem to share a romantic connection. However, his consistent show of love and loyalty means the world to me.

We still communicate daily with an inspirational quote or just a hello, his way of letting me know he's thinking of me. He throws in talk, from time to time, about how if I would visit, he would suck, lick and dick me down all night long. The offer is tempting but I can hear the alarm going off in the back of my head…Warning!

I want him to find that special woman closer to him because he's such a nice guy with a huge heart. He deserves someone that will appreciate all the love he has to offer. It's so hard nowadays to find true friendship and loyalty. Both are absolutely needed in my life.

Chapter 18

Kirkpatrick, 48, from Virginia, a retired Army sergeant, and a master mechanic for a well-known car dealership. We clicked on the site and decided to take it a step further and exchange numbers. He's another one I should have written about in my first book because he and I have been communicating for about 2 years now.

Before we spoke on the phone, I was thinking since he was from up top, I was going to get some New York flavor. To my surprise, he had an accent like he was from the south, plus he had a gold tooth to match the voice, LOL!

He was humorous besides being handsome, 6'0, caramel-coated and you can tell he worked out often by his muscular frame. We started off slow. I wasn't really for a relationship at that time, plus I didn't want another long distance fling. If I wanted to go out to dinner or on a date, I would have to jump on a plane or drive miles down the highway to enjoy a man's company. He knew he had it going on because he sent me numerous full body and dick pictures every week. No shirt, dick posing from all angles, bath scenes, dressed in suits, standing up in the mirror as if he was superman. By him being so physically fit, he was a show off and he wasn't short in the dick department either.

I definitely met him at a time when I was feeling low and his shoulder and ears were available to me anytime I needed someone to talk to. His pictures left nothing to the imagination.

We were making plans to meet and spend some quality time together but our work schedules wouldn't allow it. I know the visit would be worth my while and not a waste of time. But on the other hand, I didn't want to be sprung, gaining frequent flyer points and miles on my car,

LOL! We truly connected in more ways than one. We'd both had close family deaths, both mental and physical setbacks, and divorces from unhealthy relationships.

Months into us talking on the phone, I still had my active online account and so did he, which wasn't a problem. We were just friends but every time I went on the site he would either call or text asking, "What are you doing?"

Either this nigga was peeking through my window or he was stalking my page. So I did the next best thing and blocked his ass, LOL!

Another quality I liked in him was his faith in God and prayer. That was a bonus and helped us continue our phone friendship. He was respectful, for the most part, throwing a curve ball in the game by requesting sexy or nude pictures daily. He would play it off by adding a LOL or an emoji at the end of his text, just to see what my reaction or response would be and if I was down for the sex games through video chatting. I broke down, sending him some eye catching, mouth watering, sexy scenes. That "make you wanna slap your momma"type shit. LMAO!!!!

Don't get me wrong, he was eye candy with at least 8 inches of thickness under his belt, but the issue still remained, **DISTANCE.**

We were searching for mutual video chat apps and I asked if he had the most popular one, he stated he wasn't on there. Time marched on.

On one particular day, as I was on the social media page scrolling, I noticed they had a section called "Who You May Know". You know what happened next? Wait for it... Wait for it. Take a wild guess. Of course! His black ass had a page on the same popular social media site. You remember the one he said he wasn't on.

So I go on his "non-existent" page and he had some religious frames around some of his photos. I go down a little more and he's praising a bishop that he probably worships with every Sunday. My first thought was, *Why would he lie,* as if he had something to hide. I didn't see anything suspicious, so I'm wondering what's his reason for lying? HAHA! Bingo!!!!

The month we started chatting, he was all hugged up, in matching outfit, taking professional pictures I guess with his woman. He didn't have to hide that from me, we weren't together physically, just a mental friendship between 2 adults. I always believed when you lie it's to cover up something you don't want someone to know. It kind of hurt my feelings because he didn't have to lie to me and now my trust was gone as well.

I called him, asking "Are you a minister and why did you lie about having the page?"

"No, I'm not a preacher and I haven't used that page." Well, I'll be damned!!!

His alley cat, hush puppy wearing, orange juice drinking, Steve Harvey suit having , Lil Wayne gold yuck mouth, lemon head, funny-shaped dome on his shoulders having, casket sharp velvet curtain jacket wearing, wanna be a porn star dreaming ASS was cold busted. We stopped talking and didn't hear from each other for months. I don't want to associate with people that lie because they can't be trusted.

After about 5-6 months passed, I received a group chain letter about telling the one you love, before it's too late, that you love them, from him. Not knowing how to respond, I waited for a few minutes and told him thank you for thinking of me. That opened the door for him to vent and tell me how much he missed me and how he didn't realize how much he loved me until he lost our friendship. I could identify and agree with that. When you are in a routine or habit of talking to someone, a certain set of emotions and admiration can begin to grow for that person. I admitted I missed him as well and had love in my heart for his lousy ass. We picked up where we left off, not missing a beat.

I honestly can say I do love him. Where we may end up, who knows. We talk/text daily and express our love hours on end…

Chapter 19

Another loving friendship I formed was with Tyler from New York. An army veteran who was injured while serving this country to near death, but by the grace of God and with extensive rehab, he survived.

From the start of our meeting online, we hit it off but just as friends. Our conversations on and offline were always respectable, nurturing, and sincere.

Tyler is a father of four, a social services representative for veterans and their spouses, and a future political representative for the state of New York. Tyler is a great guy with a greater heart for everyone he comes in contact with. Always sacrificing, sometimes not even eating lunch to better serve and provide the veterans and spouses the benefits they deserve. I think that is what attracted me to him the most, he was always helping others and playing the sole parental role 7 days a week for the better good of his children.

We talked weekly for over a year. He was my shoulder to cry on, he encouraged me to be the best I can be and live with no regrets, and prayed for me and the kids daily; for our safety and that no harm come upon us at any time.

The first of the year, his birthday was approaching so making plans to visit was a no-brainer. In preparing for his birthday, I made him one of my famous gift boxes with the Chicago vs. New York theme. The inside contained a set made by Kenneth Cole, a Chicago Cubs jacket and champagne. He in turn bought us Broadway show tickets to see "**Jitney**" in Times Square and provided the hotel suite.

He picked me up from the airport looking just as I expected because we'd video chatted numerous times. We decided to have lunch since we had time before the room was ready. We parked, got out of the car and that's when I noticed our height difference. I thought he was taller.

As we walked towards the restaurant, he dragged his left leg and held his left arm in an upright position. I was taken aback because all this time, he'd never shared the severity of his injuries. Not that it made a difference, I just didn't know. I was shocked.

We sat and talked about the details of his injuries, surgeries and near death experience. I was so proud of him for never allowing his disability to slow him down and kill his spirit. Now I understood why he goes so hard for other veterans and their families.

We checked into the hotel, relaxed a little and popped bottles of champagne preparing for our evening in

Manhattan. Traffic was the pits! It took us 3 hours to get from Queens to Manhattan thinking we had missed the play but the angels were on our side. Finding a place to park and walking blocks to the theater was difficult besides being overcrowded. The weather was descent, and with his injuries, I had to grab his arm to maneuver through the throng before they knocked him down.

The theater had a lot of history. I was excited not knowing what to expect, seeing this was my first Broadway play. The show was very interesting. "**Jitney**" by August Wilson the one who wrote "**Fences**." Our evening was a blast and we fought our way back to Queens and called it a night.

Next morning/afternoon we got up, had breakfast, both a little worn from the previous day so we decided to chill. I found a liquor store, bought champagne and enjoyed our evening talking the night away.

Up, up and away, time for me to get back to the Windy City. I really enjoyed getting away, that's number one. Number two, to see and spend time with my friend for his birthday was awesome. Number three, seeing a Broadway play and making it home safely was the ultimate.

The lesson I learned was the Lord brings people in your life for a reason. Everyone I have met online is not for intimacy but for a much more powerful source, one that is long-lasting and genuine. Friendship and genuine love, I cherish both these qualities in him. He's near and dear, close to my heart.

Chapter 20

At this point in my life, I decided to sit back and allow the Lord to do his duty. I made up my mind... that was my last flight for love. I was not going across the states looking for Mr. Goodbar, he would have to be willing to come see me or live in Illinois.

With that being said, I connected with someone that was in a popular social media group, who eased their way into my inbox and my heart. I received a message one day from this man I've never seen or recalled meeting before, saying hello. The normal routine when someone requests me as a 'friend' or leaves me an inbox, is for me to go to their profile to see who we have in common. We shared a common associate. So I thought nothing of it and asked him,

"Where did we meet?"

He responded with, "I thought we may have met at a party." BAAAAAAAAAhhhhhhh!!!!!!!!

Anyone that really knows me knows I don't hang out or do much partying these days. LOL! I went with it and we messaged each other weekly, checking on each other's well-being and weekly activities. We became friends on the site and began commenting and liking each other's posts, no big deal.

Dillan was 45, 5'10, musician/producer, and a father. Our friendship blossomed month after month and shifted after 3 months of communicating. I was at the crossroad of wanting a relationship or being single. I had been single for about 1 ½ years at this point, plus my past long distance relationship carried on over 2 years and we only saw each other a few times a year. It's safe to say I'd been by myself a long time and had grown accustom to being alone.

After these months of continuous flirting, we decided to finally meet in person a day before I was moving my mom to Las Vegas. I threw on a dress and met him in a neighborhood grocery parking lot. I parked, we embraced each other as if we'd known one another for years. We saw each other through Face Time but to have the person in front of you is a totally different reality. The touch, smell, and feel of someone rolls over into the mental part of the bond you are sharing. With promises of meeting for an extended visit, we parted ways,

Attempts at hooking up when I returned from Vegas were fruitless. Our schedules wouldn't gel. He worked 7 days a week, yes 7, plus I had an upcoming event I'd put my all into but the fulfillment of our second meeting was in the making.

A couple of times I tried to stop talking to him as much, but it seemed pointless; he wouldn't have it. Reason being, if I couldn't foresee happiness for myself why waste time? He assured me I wasn't. We eventually made time for each other, meeting up at a hotel in separate cars. I called to get directions to the room.

As I was walking across the grass, the strap on my sandal broke. OMG! I could barely walk, the sandal kept going sideways and I was trying to grip my foot to hold it in place. Galloping my way down the hall like a clumsy ass horse, I finally made it to the room and was embarrassed. I entered the room, we hugged and sat on opposite sides of the bed. I began talking, probably too much. I'm shy and can admit when I'm nervous. I can be a bit chatty, LOL! (I know y'all saying, her ass ain't shy. LMAO!!). I guess he got tired of talking, came over to my side and kissed me in my mouth like he meant that shit. Of course I joined in the tongue struggle. He laid on top of me. Please note, I hadn't had any male attention for a minute, so really I was satisfied.

Still clothed, he ground his hard dick up against my moist pussy; this was my thing. I immediately came, and then he asked me if I enjoyed it? My answer was on my face. He lifted my dress and removed my lace panties and spread my thick thighs apart like the red sea. He began sucking all around my juicy ass pussy like he had been there before. This nigga knew where, when, and just how much pressure to apply with each lick, suck, and twirl of his tongue all up in me. DAMN!!! Before you knew it, I was cummin' the second time. WTF!!!...

After he seductively slurped up my nectar, I scooted back on the bed, trying to get my composure together. I laid on my stomach as he began massaging me from my shoulders to my ass then he got on my back. Remember, we still had on clothes.

He began kissing the back of my neck, squeezing my nipples and grinding his hard dick up against my ass. I was in heat. He got off the bed and stood as I turned to watch the strip. I couldn't wait to see what he was working with.

His dick was pointing straight out like a tent. When that muthafucka pulled out that pretty thick ass dick, my mouth instantly watered and eyes got big as bow dollars. A solid, strong body attached to this great piece of dick with them full thick lips. I could read the writing on the wall; I was in for the fuck of my life. He wrapped his dick in that magnum condom and it was time to put in that work.

As he entered my tight walls, just giving me one inch at time, it felt like heaven and the angels were singing. LMAO!!! He gave me that dick like a CHAMP! Stroke for stroke I was hanging with that ass. I wasn't no punk. I was throwing that wet pussy right back at him. Our rhythm was like clockwork, the sounds of my wetness as he was holding my thighs back going deeper in my pussy was like

music to his ears. I was giving him pound for pound and

enjoying every inch of it!

Chapter 21

The scene was sexy as hell as we interlocked fingers winding ass muscles back and forth as if we were on a water bed. His dick control was off the chain! He was not quitting until he put it all inside me to let me know he'd been in this pussy. Challenge!!! I was tired as hell, LOL!!!...Uh, Uh my turn.

I told him to lay on his back. I took in the sight of his beautiful body, strong hands, broad shoulders, and his thick round suckable mushroom head. I licked and sucked the tasty ass juices from my sweet pussy as I kissed his mouth, then went back to work slobbing and sucking as much dick as I could get in my mouth. He was big so I grabbed it with one hand, going up and down, sucking it at the same time, driving him to ecstasy.

Next, I sat my round ass on top of him and spread my ass cheeks so he could feel all of this good pussy. I worked that thick pole like my life depended on it, round and round, up and down and went in for the kill. Easing off the dick and slow grinding down in a spiral until it was in my deepness. We began to cum together. I kissed him in his mouth, taking in every huff and puff of air he took as he let out his creamy nut. We ended side by side, breathing heavily and looking into each other eyes with satisfaction, declaring how good our session was.

We continued to pillow talk for a few moments, then out of nowhere, this mug pulled my pussy into his mouth, lifting my ass in air. I was so outdone as I melted with wide spread thighs, welcoming his hungry mouth. My pussy grinding into the creamy puddle as I came hard into his mouth, thighs shaking and him not missing a drop of my juices. Next, he swiftly slid on another Magnum then eased into my wetness again.

Later that evening, while talking on the phone, he stated he couldn't stop thinking of me and the feeling was mutual. I haven't been dicked down like that in a long ass time. I was a happy camper. Curled up like a baby sucking her thumb. Don't play with me. LOL!!!

Baaaabbbbyyyy! I tried to sit up in my bed to get out of it and I was sore as hell!!! I felt every muthafuckin' muscle from my shoulders to the top of my feet. It felt like I got my ass whooped! Even my stomach muscles felt like I'd been doing crunches, LOL! I had to swing my legs over the side of the bed to get out of it. I could barely walk. This nigga fucked me royally and I fucked him right back with everything I had in me.

I had a lot of errands to run but I was jacked up. I was barely able to sit on the toilet to pee. Just after a certain point of trying to ease down, I just had to plop my ass down. My pussy was sore, my lips from kissing him were sore, my whole body was sore, but I was satisfied. Even on the day of my event, I was still moving in slow motion as if he was still inside me. I enjoyed every minute of his aggressive ass, although it took me a few days to get myself together.

We continued our friendship but I knew I was setting myself up to be hurt because he couldn't give me the relationship I deserved and wanted. I was cautious but my heart wasn't.

Chapter 22

We confessed feelings for each other, wanting the best for one another but knew our love was forbidden. Sometimes you can't help who you fall for. His first love was his career. I knew spending time trying to be a regular boyfriend would be challenging for him. He traveled around the world playing and making music in all arenas; this was before me, and it would be after me. I would get frustrated and tell him not to call or block him. He would get upset and we would talk and be cool again.

Our base and love as friends was strong but a relationship was a roller coaster. I fell weak for da D-I-C-K (in my Eryka Badu voice) and rode the muthafucka like it was the last piece of good dick on this earth. Of course it was the bomb; our love making wasn't the issue; we fit like a glove.

After the last go around, I decided to separate myself and blocked him for a month or so, just to get him out my system. But sho' as my name is Catrina Danette Brown, he contacts me and our love still stands. I will always cherish our times, talks, trust and respect for each other but I can't cry over spilled milk.

Chapter 23

Next, I spoke to Sean. He was 43, 6'2, fine, a suburban police officer and thick like I like 'em. MmmMmm...

We met a couple of years back on the site, only talking briefly. We also shared a couple of friends on a social media sites but didn't connected initially. It just hadn't been OUR time.

Throughout the past year, we used a video walkie-talkie like site to speak or flirt, depending on our mood, to keep our momentum going. He caught me on an off day, asking me out to lunch. I joined him and it was good to finally be in each other's presence. We enjoyed great food, laughter and spirits and at the end of our lunch, in the parking lot, he asked to come by for some cocktails. In my R. Kelly voice my mind was telling me NO!!! But my body, BODY!!! Is telling me YESSS!!! LOL!! Ain't nothing wrong with a little bump and grind…I need to quit.

As I was following him, I realized he lived only 20 minutes from my place. He was a bachelor with dogs so you know I was scared to go in but he assured me they were put up. I was impressed; he had a nice, clean house. If he didn't tell you he had dogs, you wouldn't have known it.

His home had a loft feel with a fireplace, deck and all the modern amenities. We sat in the family room watching a little TV while chitchatting about our life moments and sipping cocktails. Once he wrapped his strong arm around me and planted those big juicy ass lips on mine, it was on. Kissing is my thing; it's sensual.

Our tongues were dancing with a rhythm like no other, and my juicy tongue tracing the outline of his lips as

I suck on the bottom one slowly and real soft. Sweetly jamming your tongue inside his wet mouth and sucking his tongue like a dick, in and out side to side. Slurping all that seeps out the side of his mouth as you are sucking his soul into yours. Breathing sweetness into his hot willing mouth, up for anything my body yearned. He lifted me up and escorted me into his bedroom; candles lit and soft music playing while in my mind thinking this youngin' had his shit together.

As we kissed each other lightly removing a piece of clothing from each other's overheated bodies, the intensity of our passion grew as the last piece dropped, looking hungrily into each other's eyes. It was on like a pot of neck bones, LMAO!!!

He laid me down onto the center of his bed and laid on top of my softness and began grinding his hardness into me until it found its way into my wet juicy pussy. We fucked each other pound for pound until we came together, reaching one common goal, a long-lasting orgasm. He rolled over breathless. I got up, asking for a towel and the bathroom. I got myself together, got dressed and again thanked him for a great afternoon. I'm not one for laying up in somebody's house all day and night; I got my own. We kissed goodnight until the next episode.

Days and weeks passed with our friendship still intact, not getting it twisted because we fucked. With our work schedules, family, etc., we will continue enjoying each other's company when time permits. "Friends till the end."

Chapter 24

Then popped up Ronald. He left a few messages in my box but I wasn't interested because his profile stated he was legally separated. That's a 'no-no' but I understood getting a jump start on your new life, especially when your relationship has been over for a minute.

We chatted casually on and off on the site while stressing to him that nothing could become of us because of his status. He said he respected and honored my word, besides he wasn't looking for sex he wanted a friend. So we had an understanding. We talked daily, check up on each other's day, and fuss about our jobs.

I met him at a time in my life when I wasn't very happy. I was going through depression, not liking my job, and my room became my comfort zone. He could identify since he had been in his career over 20 years and was not very happy with his job either. He had one daughter, had been married for 20 years, owned a lot of real estate and had traveled around the world and back; all with his wife.

He said they fell out of love years ago but his love of his daughter wouldn't allow him to leave. They were transitioning between homes so eventually she could adjust to them not being together. I would talk and he would give me advice.

One day, out the blue, he said, "Your life has been so interesting you should write a book." LOL! When I told him I had, he could have hit the floor. He Googled my information and was amazed that everything we talked about was in my book. He praised me for being a great writer with an even greater story to tell. Our bond was like brother and sister, we had a growing admiration for one another.

A month later we decided to meet in person one Saturday night. We met for cocktails, and it was like we'd known each other for years. He was a couple inches taller than me, dressed nice and smelled good as hell. I love a man that smells good. We drank and laughed until the wee hours of the morning. I had to work in the a.m. so we parted.

Our friendship grew more and more each day, even making plans to travel to see one of my favorite artists with the intent on getting separate rooms. I have learned the Lord brings people in your life for a reason. Also, everyone is not made for an intimate relationship but you can love someone without physical interaction.

We had lunch one afternoon in Hyde Park like old friends. Afterwards, we parted, going our separate way to enjoy ourselves at family gatherings. However, later that evening we did talk and I could see myself in him. I told him he needed to slow down drinking; he gets a little beside himself plus he was driving. Now I understood when people would tell me to slow down. I finally got it.

I got home, checked my messages on the site and low and behold, guess who I see? Ronald! My buddy I'd just had lunch with and been talking to for 2 months. He'd changed the status on his profile to Divorced. In one spot, he'd reiterated in bold writing FINALLY DIVORCED!!!

I called him, he was still hanging with his family so I asked him to give me a couple of minutes, I wanted to talk to him. I sent him a picture of his profile, with his updated information, and I told him he didn't have to lie to me. We are friends and trust and loyalty mean everything to me. He explained he did that to get numbers for a friend because he wasn't getting responses with his profile as it was... BULLSHIT!!!

Chapter 25

We didn't talk for a day or two because I can't stand liars. He finally called, asking if we could talk. I said okay because I don't hold grudges, I just know how you are now. He left work and we met at a Japanese hibachi grill. The food was fantastic and the cocktails were better. I told him we were cool and we enjoyed our night.

After dinner, we stopped by Pepe's for more drinks. I ordered a Blue Motherfucker and he had a martini. I promise you, I don't know if I had 1 or 2 more, but The DEAD had risen, TRIXIE was back in full effect.

We got back to the car, acting just like teenagers and we didn't have a care in the world. People were walking past the car and we didn't give a fuck; we were over the top.

"This isn't going to work..." I whispered ".. let's go to my house."

My sons were home so going in was out. I parked my car in my garage, went inside the house and changed my clothes. I put on a t-shirt and shorts for easy access.

When I arrived back to the garage, we started kissing, rubbing and touching; our bodies were on fire. I sat in a lawn chair, spread my thick thighs apart and he went to work.

He was sucking and slurping on my juicy pussy like it was a Georgia peach. I started cummin and squirting with every touch of his tongue on my clit. I unzipped his jeans, pulled out his dick and went to town. I sucked the head of his dick, in and out of my hot mouth until he couldn't take it anymore. Before he came, I turned my ass around, grabbed my ankles and stuck his dick in my wet pussy like it was a vacuum cleaner. We fucked into the wee hours of the morning and several fulfilling orgasms. We got ourselves together and bid each other a good morning.

For the next hours to daylight, I couldn't go to sleep, I was drunk as hell and embarrassed. I couldn't even go to work. I was like *Trina, what did you do?* That went all against what I stood for with him being separated, divorced, or whatever.

For days we didn't talk or text. He said he had a death in his family in another state and that was cool because I did not want to face him, ever, after our encounter. It was wrong and the Lord surely did punish me for that act. My gotdamn knee has been fucked up ever since LMAO!!!!!! He taught me a lesson, NO MARRIED MEN!!!

A couple of months later, he called me out the blue, apologizing for his actions, and saying he missed and still loved me. I thought I was getting punked. Where did this come from? I accepted his apology and told him we were good. Just another lesson, remember no regrets.

Chapter 26

The 3 + 1 Jersey boo's; let me explain. I met and talked to 3 different men from New Jersey but they lived in different parts of the city. The + one was another guy from New Jersey I met a week after talking to each one of the other 3.

Ronnie was a business owner, father, and very intelligent man. In his pictures, he dressed nice but physically he was not my type (he resembled my father). I love to hear him speak and not just for his accent. I was intrigued by his in-depth knowledge as well.

We talked for a few weeks, hours on end, until one night he must have had a few too many. He caught Trixie on the right night. I was ready to play.

He said he was stroking his big dick real nice and slow, waiting for me to sit my wet pussy on his pole. He continued on about how he was going to suck my clit until I squirted in his mouth with all my succulent juices. I joined in the fun, telling him I was going to lick and stroke the head of his dick until he exploded. We really went hard that night and it was hilarious!

His ability to get my attention was to die for. I had a death in the family and he showed generous concern and compassion. I would never forget that about him.

After our phone sex, I didn't hear from him for a couple of days which was odd. I text him and told him it was okay and he didn't have anything to be embarrassed about. This punk text me back and said the reason he hadn't called was because he had the flu. Also, he was glad this happened before he got into me because I was sending him crazy ass messages. I took the high road and I text back, sending the peace sign. However, I started to tell that Kermit the frog looking muthafucka about himself, LOL!!!

Clay 6'3, fine as hell, and a stallion, was 43 with no kids. He had his own house, cars, motorcycles and 2 big ass dogs he loved like they were his kids. He was a beast, a no-nonsense type of guy. We connected but in the back of my mind his age and arrogance played a part in deterring me from getting to know him better. He told me if he came to visit me in Chicago, he wasn't staying in a hotel, he was staying at my house. Ta-he-he hell! Him staying at my house with my kids was a no-no. I knew I couldn't give him children and I knew he wasn't going to be the boss of me; someone would definitely get the short end of that stick.

What threw me off guard with him was his level of insecurity for a man that had everything. Sometimes, when I meet people, I know when I have to hold and definitely when I have to fold. If I missed a call and didn't return it or called the next day, he would be in his feelings and have an attitude. He would question why I didn't respond in a timely manner or accuse me of being too busy to have him in my life. I knew it wasn't a Keith Sweat "Make it Last Forever" moment. LMAO!!!!

Tom was 55, distinguished, a former overseas NBA player, high yellow, and easy on the eyes. He was employed in the IT field and an adamant golfer. I was impressed with his profile and I reached out to him, leaving a flirty message that he'd caught my eye.

We clicked instantly. He was funny, caring, and an undercover freak. Weeks turned into months of talking, then he asked about the nearest airport and hotel.

Chapter 27

I was impressed with Tom. He had his own house in Brooklyn, his own money, and in time, eventually wanted to take us to another level. Our friendship and communication grew with each day. I looked forward to hearing his voice, reading his sweet texts, and enjoying our 'face time' moments. He was very comfortable with us.

He would pop up on my phone with his dick in his hand on any given day. He didn't have a problem stroking that curved dick, which is just the right size to please a sister. I told him that bow-legged ass dick was a bonus for my g-spot. We would tease each other with promises of the best fuck of our lives. That impressed me because very few would say "I'll come see you..."

I didn't doubt we could be good together but in the back of my mind, I was thinking, *Am I really equipped for another long distance relationship?* I did know I was ready for a relationship near or far. We will see if he's still in the running. Mister plus 1, I don't know what it is about that New York/New Jersey flavor. It makes me wanna slap my momma. LOL!!!

Chapter 28

Next up was Bobby; we worked in similar fields, social services. We both understood and respected our positions. When working in an institution with mental/criminal elements, as soon as you hit the floor, it is 'showtime'.

He had 2 adult children and had his own everything. He could dress up in a suit and tie and take it back down in the streets in his Tim's. He was okay to talk to but it felt awkward at times because some of our conversations seemed forced; they didn't flow naturally. He was caramel, handsome, confident, and he favored the 90's singer, Case. In a way, I was deterred from becoming serious with someone from another state. It sounds crazy, but those are the men I make better connections with.

He made a great effort to talk to me but we just didn't click. He would 'FaceTime' me at any given moment, I guess to see if I was alone. CLOWN! Tricks are for kids, silly rabbit.

I wish him all the best. It just wasn't in the cards for us. My first rule of thumb is: if you take time out to leave me a personal message 9 out of 10 times, out of respect, I will respond.

Chapter 29

Randy was easy on the eyes but reminded me of the man in the 7-eleven saying, "Welcome to 7-eleven, how may I help you?" LMAO!!!!! He'd sent me a flirt or two previously. Why we never connected? Not really sure.

On this particular day, he sent me a message asking, "You haven't gotten married yet?"

"No, I'm waiting patiently for the man the Lord is preparing for me."

He said, "I've been trying but you never gave me your time."

He definitely caught my attention with his remark so I went back to our first exchange of words. It was almost a year prior. That should have been my first sign. I shook it off as he was persistent.

That afternoon we began chatting back and forth as he intrigued me with his charm and confidence. He said, "I will never give up on you and let's not block our blessing this time."

I told him I was open to having a relationship minus the extra games, lies, and shenanigans." After weeks communicating, I discovered he was sweet, loving and a promising candidate in my world. He was employed, a father, and had his own, but he lacked in trust. I didn't blame him. It's a lot of liars, manipulators, married men, and cheaters on the site; so trust just can't be given, it has to be earned.

We continued learning each other but he would make odd comments and even asked me to meet his mother. I didn't know people still did that. He would tell me if he couldn't have me, nobody could because I was his future. I think I fell for the attention and the idea of having a prince charming with promises of everlasting love and happiness.

At that point in my life, I was accepting the fact I might remain single for the rest of my days. For someone to try to prove me wrong was a challenge, although I was okay with being single.

After a month or so of talking and video chatting, we met up and I was looking sexy as hell. That first impression may be your last. I pulled up, getting out my car with a mini dress and 3-inch heels to match. He got out and was 3 inches shorter than me. LOL! I felt like a damn Amazon. LMAO!!! I wanted to take my shoes off right then and there just to see if we were the same height. We hugged and it felt so natural, as if we'd known each other forever.

He was crazy as hell in a funny kind of way and would tell me in a minute, "Quit trying to stop talking to me. I am not letting you go so cut it out."

On our next date, we hung out and had dinner. It was part of the process of getting to know one another better. Being as it was a work day, we ended it early and said our good nights. I can honestly say I needed someone to tell me to go sit my ass down somewhere sometimes, so I was up for the challenge. We continued to talk/text daily and go out on dates whenever our schedules permitted.

One Sunday, we met for breakfast. The food and company was the bomb. I followed him back to his place; for a bachelor, it was a really nice place. He offered me a key and an open invitation whenever I wanted to just come by. We kissed and rubbed, pieces of clothing vanishing one at a time as we looked into each other eyes. We made love to each other mind, body and soul, the sensual intimacy and passion was just natural.

Listening to Lalah as we laid in the afterglow of our union, caressing each other into an afternoon slumber. This was a shock to me; feeling comfortable enough around someone to rest without taking a sleeping pill.

For the following week, we continued seeing one another, with me going over to his place. He would leave the door open for me if he stepped out. It made me feel a little more trusting but his desire to control my every move weren't as easy to deal with.

Our intimacy, communication, and sense of security were on the same page and I definitely felt more at ease. I will admit, I had champagne plus a little Trixie, so that did not mix for an easy night. Our sex was the bomb with some additional sucking each other off.

Even after becoming sober and the reality of the previous night, I didn't show my ass and I was not wearing my red shoes and including my Bozo red nose. LMAO!! I don't know if it was my sleeping pills or GOD…. I got my ass up and out of his in place in 2.2 seconds. Honestly leaving and driving was a dumb move on my part. I could have hurt myself or anyone that was in my path on the expressway while attempting to make it home safely.

We talked on and off after that but I didn't want to continue; call it cold feet or whatever. I didn't feel he was the one. I told him I was bowing out gracefully and continued blessings.

He said, "You are unpredictable. You're one way and minutes or days later you're another."

We were at a crossroad. We were both still talking to other people. He may have been doing more than that but I'm not sure. He had someone that liked him or vice versa and once I discovered that, I pulled out. I wouldn't want anyone stringing me along or playing with my heartstrings. I told him good-bye, final chapter.

A few weeks passed with no communication. I was at work when he called and said..

"Hello Ms. Brown." I spoke back.

He went on to say, "I told my best friend Michelle about you."

I replied, "What did you tell her?"

"She's on the phone."

"Hey Michelle. I've heard so much about you."

Michelle responded with, "I've heard a lot about you as well. That's all he talks about."

"See Michelle, I have to call her at work because she blocked me on her phone."

"The phone I pay for every month. Of course, we are not dealing with each other. What is there to talk about?" I responded with some heat. "I'm not a game-player and my time is very precious to me. I have no regrets; we good, we just move differently."

"Well, he is single," Michelle added her two cents.

"So am I."

She said, "Did your feelings change?"

"No, but his got deeper."

Michelle just kept coming, "People may say things because they think that's what you want to hear."

Hold up wait minute! Now, it was time to go in CHECK mode and teach her about the REAL CATRINA.

I said, "There was no need for false promises or lies. No one has to promise me marriage; been there, it just didn't work out. I'm at peace with us and he should just move on because I don't misuse or take advantage of people. That's not my character. It's bad karma and it comes back to bite you in your ass."

The funny thing is, the whole time we were talking, this punk was quiet as hell.

He finally joins in and says, "I want you to know I really liked you."

He then asked about my upcoming event and mentioned he still planned on coming.

I said, "Okay, and Michelle, I invited you as well."

"I'll try to make it."

I went on to say, "You all have a blessed day," and ended the conversation. If that wasn't the craziest shit in the world? What the fuck did they think, they were going to double team me about why I stopped talking to him? I couldn't understand for the life of me why he would call me at my job, number one, and with his best friend on the phone for number two. If he'd had another shot, he blew it with that childish mess. He lost all cool points for that move.

The next day he called me at work again. "Good morning, Ms. Brown. I hope you don't mind me calling your job; it's because you still have me blocked." UNBELIEVABLE!!! The other line rang and. I told him to hold on. Eventually he hung up. I guess I took too long to come back or the light finally clicked on and he realized he could be taped and charged for continually calling my job.

My coworkers were hyped. They were waiting for him to call back so they could cuss his ass out.

"You got a stalker and we're going to tell his ass don't call here no motherfuckin' more." LMAO!!!

All jokes aside, his actions were unstable. It made me uneasy and his behavior couldn't be trusted. After work, I unblocked him to notify him with one final warning; not to ever call my job. He didn't answer the call so I text him and he responded with an apology. He said he just wanted to let me know he loved me and always will. He then asked if it was possible to meet up and talk to him. Hell to tha' Naw Naw!! I may be blonde but I'm not a dumb blonde. There was nothing else to discuss. For his sake, I pray he takes heed to my warning. I have dealt with some 'nuts' in my lifetime and when people become obsessed with you, someone can get hurt. That's why I don't play with people's heartstrings. They will either hurt you because they feel if they can't they have you no one else can. You don't know what frame of mind a person can be in.

Having multiple on and off relationships or friendships through the site, I was hoping and praying I would have found the love of my life by now. As it stands, I am single and at peace with me and the choices I have made. I continue daily to work on a better me. How can I expect someone to be in order if I'm still finding my way?

I'm going on a hiatus from the online dating scene. It can be discouraging, continually meeting people to see if he is the one. The process of dating can be overwhelming; getting to know someone new, their values, the way they communicate best, favorite food, favorite color, or what kind of relationship they are seeking. I'm at the point where I no longer give a damn. LOL!

Seriously, I'm not giving up, just sitting back, relaxing and waiting to see who's still standing when the smoke clears. He's still out there somewhere…

About The Author

Catrina D. Brown, author of .CUM, a book on the reality of online dating, is the mother of 3 sons, 1 daughter (R.I.H.), and one granddaughter. She has worked in the law enforcement field for over 24 years with over 4 years experience using online dating services.

She has met men all over the United States via chat, text, video chatting, phone or even in person. She is a real person, with a real heart, looking for a real relationship, not just one to write about.

Catrina travels from city to city and state to state in search of her one true love. Her belief is the Lord is preparing her for the man she deserves. Not knowing when and where, she continues to step out on faith for her final chapter.

Catrina Brown

Author of .CUM and Guess Who's Cummin?

www.ingramcontent.com/pod-product-compliance
Lightning Source LLC
Chambersburg PA
CBHW030654110726
47901CB00002B/709